MARGARITA ENGLE

ART BY BEATRIZ GUTIERREZ HERNANDEZ

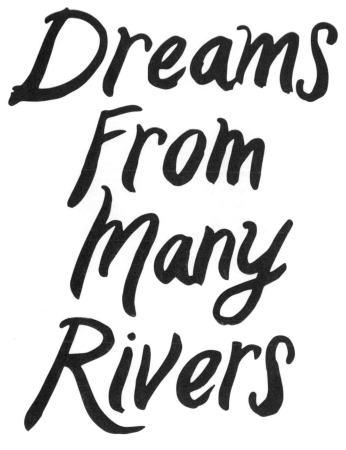

Dreams From Many Rivers

**A HISPANIC HISTORY OF THE
UNITED STATES TOLD IN POEMS**

GODWIN BOOKS

HENRY HOLT AND COMPANY · NEW YORK

*For young people whose rivers of dreams
are so varied and hopeful
and for Laura Godwin with gratitude*

Henry Holt and Company, *Publishers since 1866*
Henry Holt® is a registered trademark of Macmillan Publishing Group, LLC
120 Broadway, New York, New York 10271 • mackids.com

Library of Congress Cataloging-in-Publication Data
Names: Engle, Margarita, author. | Gutierrez, Beatriz (Gutierrez Hernandez), illustrator.
Title: Dreams from many rivers : a Hispanic history of the United States told in poems /
    Margarita Engle ; illustrated by Beatriz Gutierrez.
Description: First edition. | New York : Godwin Books, Henry Holt and Company, [2019] |
    Includes historical note.
Identifiers: LCCN 2019002542 | ISBN 9781627795319 (hardcover)
Subjects: LCSH: Hispanic Americans—History—Juvenile poetry. | Children's poetry, American.
Classification: LCC PS3555.N4254 A6 2019 | DDC 811/.54—dc23
LC record available at https://lccn.loc.gov/2019002542

Our books may be purchased in bulk for promotional, educational, or business use. Please
contact your local bookseller or the Macmillan Corporate and Premium Sales Department at
(800) 221-7945 ext. 5442 or by email at MacmillanSpecialMarkets@macmillan.com.

First edition, 2019 / Designed by Carol Ly

Printed in the United States of America by LSC Communications, Harrisonburg, Virginia
10 9 8 7 6 5 4 3 2 1

HISTORICAL NOTE

Most US history books begin with colonization of the thirteen colonies by English invaders who conquered numerous Indigenous nations. However, the part of modern US territory that was colonized the earliest is Puerto Rico. As a result, Hispanic history in regions that are now called the United States spans more than five centuries. In addition, the Indigenous ancestry of mestizos on modern US territory extends for tens of thousands of years, and includes countless nations from all the Américas: North, South, and Central. Condensing every aspect into one book of poems would be an overwhelming task. All I've tried to do in *Dreams from Many Rivers* is portray a few glimpses of a vast and complicated past.

With the exception of the first section about Borikén (Puerto Rico), I have used modern place names to avoid confusion since historically, place names changed quite often.

Only Hispanic and Latino voices are included in *Dreams from Many Rivers*, with the exception of Indigenous Taíno voices in the first section. Fictional characters are indicated by first name only, while historical figures include a surname or title.

I have made no attempt to explain the history and politics of countries of origin of US Latinos, because they include dozens of Latin American countries, as well as many other parts of the world.

Television programs, movies, and popular culture often portray Latinos as impoverished *barrio* dwellers. The truth is that we live in every part of the United States, both rural and urban; poor, middle class, and wealthy. Our reasons for living in the United States range from being here before it became the US to arriving as refugees or arriving as highly qualified doctors, scientists, artists, and musicians. We are complex. We cannot be simplified.

In order to write about US Latino history, I had to make two essential decisions. The first was facing the shameful atrocities of Spanish conquistadors and their descendants, including invasions, genocide, conquest, forced labor, persecution, and racism. Spanish invaders were just as brutal as English invaders, slaughtering Native Americans, enslaving the survivors, then importing enslaved people from Africa. This book is an attempt to portray our history honestly, rather than choosing to ignore the parts that we long to forget.

The second decision was acknowledging that the history of the modern US begins in Puerto Rico, not Plymouth Rock or Jamestown, as is widely believed. Puerto Ricans are US citizens. They can travel freely between the island and mainland without passports. They pay taxes. But Puerto Rico is a territory, not a state. They are not allowed to vote in presidential elections. They often have to endure being mistaken for immigrants. This dual nature of Puerto Rico, with two languages and a confusing in-between status, strikes me as significant for anyone who has ever felt simultaneously accepted and rejected.

Dreams from Many Rivers does not answer even a tiny fraction of the questions that a student might ask a teacher during Hispanic/Latino Heritage Month. I have my own series of enormous questions. Why has so much of the Latino experience been omitted from standard textbooks? Why are we so often reduced to a few absurd stereotypes? Why are invaders and conquerors glorified, while peacemakers are ignored? Why do we have to learn history's truths on our own, instead of encountering our real stories in school? How can this drastic injustice begin to change?

Y mi niñez fue toda un poema en el río,
y un río en el poema de mis primeros sueños.

And my childhood was all a poem in the river,
and a river in the poem of my first dreams.

JULIA DE BURGOS

ATLANTIC
OCEAN

PART ONE
FREEDOM

CARIBBEAN
SEA

A BRIEF INTRODUCTION TO THE NATIVE PEOPLE OF BORIKÉN

For thousands of years, the people who are now called Taíno lived by farming, fishing, hunting, singing, and dreaming of a future as free as the past. Men, women, and children believed in hope. The corners of fields held smooth sculptures to guard crops of manioc. The government was sophisticated and complex, with elaborate peacekeeping methods conducted by leaders called *kacikes*, and priests called *behikes*. On the walls of crystalline caves, beautiful designs were made by artistic hands. Enormous seagoing canoes carried visitors back and forth between Borikén (now known as Puerto Rico) and neighboring islands, such as Cuba and Quisqueya (now known as Hispaniola, which includes the Dominican Republic and Haiti). To this day, many Puerto Ricans still refer to their island as Borikén or Borinquen.

COURAGE

GUACARIGUA

Borikén, 1491

My mother says watch out for sharks
in the sea, caimans in the river, hurricanes,
scorpions,
crumbling cliffs . . .

but my greatest fear
is too little adventure,
not too much.

No matter how fervently my mother worries,
I need to explore, boldly trekking along all
the wild edges
of home.

There will be time enough
for caution
when I grow old.

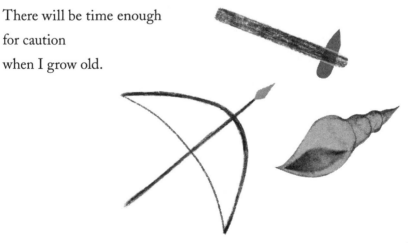

DAYDREAMS

YAIMA

Borikén, 1491

Are all little girls
just as happy
as I am
when I swim
with quiet manatees,
telling them
enchanting stories?

HUNTER

ABEY

Borikén, 1491

My work is tiring, but we need ducks
to eat and crocodiles for making tools of teeth,
bags from skin, long strips of roasted meat . . .

Land, sea, and sky feed us,
so that we're never really hungry,
except
after visits
from the guardian
of storms.

MUSIC FROM THE DEEP SEA AND HIGH SKY

GUAMO

Borikén, 1491

Mouth pressed
against a pink conch shell,
I play a song
to call
rhythms
down
from
trees,
the rattle
of palm leaves
and festive squawks
of raucous parrots
as they join
my aerial
coral-reef
melody!

THE MAGIC OF CLOTH

ALAINA AND YULURI

Borikén, 1491

Daughter and mother,
we spin and weave
cotton fibers for capes
embroidered with feathers.

Are we bird-girls?
Yes, winged creatures
of the sort children meet
on a gentle morning
of enchanting stories.

THIS PEACEFUL FARM
YABU

Borikén, 1491

I plant manioc and corn,
the gifts of life.

Each field is a sacred place
where thirsty roots drink rain
and sighing leaves chant gratitude
to the generous sky
for food.

SHAPING CLAY

ARIMA AND GUAJUMA

Borikén, 1491

Twin sisters, we take turns
forming bowls
and jars
of wet earth
with our skillful fingers.
Then we trade places, painting
designs of red and yellow minerals
on each heat-dried surface
to create the warmth
of useful ceramics,
our wealth.

MISSION SANTA CRUZ

PACIFIC OCEAN

MISSION SAN DIEGO

Alaska

Hawaii

PART TWO
SURVIVORS

Puerto Rico

ATLANTIC OCEAN

A BRIEF INTRODUCTION TO
CONQUEST AND RESISTANCE

n 1492, an Italian invader called Cristoforo Colombo (also known as Cristóbal Colón and Christopher Columbus), arrived in the so-called "new world" with Spanish soldiers, fearsome weapons, European diseases, and a desire for spices to flavor European foods.

Islanders defended their homeland, but the conquistadors were brutal newcomers who understood nothing, unable to speak any native languages or respect traditions of peace and friendship.

Men, women, and children captured by Spanish invaders in West Africa were transported to the Caribbean islands on horrific ships. Enslaved people from many African nations were forced to work alongside the enslaved Taínos. Within a few generations, hundreds of thousands of Caribbean islanders were slaughtered by weapons or disease, and most of those who survived carried a blend of Indigenous, African, and Spanish ancestry, creating a unique mixture of languages and cultures.

Meanwhile, Spanish invaders spread out in every direction, killing or enslaving millions of native people from thousands of Indigenous nations in North, Central, and South America.

CONQUEST MEANS CRUELTY

PEDRO DE ACEVEDO

Puerto Rico, 1493

As the cabin boy on this ship,
I am a witness to the excitement
of Colón, whose first journey reached
other islands.

Now, this second voyage brings us reality.
It won't be easy to find the spice trees we seek.

When I see a boy around my age,
I learn his name, Guacarigua.

He will be one of the captives,
a person enslaved.

DEFIANCE

GUACARIGUA

Puerto Rico, 1493

Our home is ours,
not theirs.

My freedom
can't be destroyed
by these monsters.

Their shields of hard metal
and those long, two-bladed knives
aren't enough to keep me
from running away
seeking
safety.

REBELLION

URAYOÁN EL CACIQUE

Puerto Rico, 1511

Invaders demand a tribute
of four golden hawk's bells
per person
per year.

The glow of yellow stone is their only greed now,
all those early demands for spice trees
completely
forgotten.

Gold nuggets have already been mined
from every river, but we are still enslaved,
and our children are dying of smallpox,
so I dream up a plan for escape by inviting
lonely soldiers to the shore of a lake,
where I promise to introduce them
to women who will be their wives.

I'm a leader, the kacike, so they believe me,
but instead of matchmaking,
I tell my people to drown a Spaniard,
and then we rise up, fighting for freedom,

until the troops of a brute called Ponce de León
attack us with cannons, lances, crossbows, muskets,
growling mastiffs,
and galloping
horses.

We have our own weapons,
light bows and arrows,
heavy war clubs,
and the weightless
sky
of
soaring
hope.

FEROCITY

JUAN PONCE DE LEÓN

Puerto Rico, 1511

My sword.
Shiny metal.
My armor.
Glittering wishes.

I seize men, women, and children
to work in the mines, but some dive into rivers
and twirl away
as swiftly
as dolphins . . .

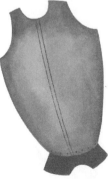

No matter, here are more.
I'll always find enough men, women, and children
to enslave, people to slice hills and mountains
in search of gold, silver, copper,
and jewels.

ESCAPE

SERAFINA

Puerto Rico, 1511

When the first Agüeybaná was alive,
he tried to get along with the brutal invaders,
showing them where to sift flakes of gold
from rivers. Then he died, and his brother
became Agüeybaná II, our rebel leader.
He almost succeeded, trying to defend
my Taíno mother's village,
where brave men and women killed hundreds
of my Spanish father's
armored soldiers.

I'm just a girl, still small enough
to slip away into the silent forest, hidden
by shadows of peaceful trees that don't care
about my two battling origins.

SURVIVAL

GUACARIGUA
Puerto Rico, 1520

The highest
most isolated
slopes.

Trickling streams instead of rushing rivers.
Stillness—then one softly whistling bird.
Or is that delicate music the song of another
survivor, pretending to be winged?

When I meet the runaway girl called Serafina,
I know that I will love her forever, and our future
will be safe here in this secret place
of sheltering trees
and hidden villages.

NEVER ENOUGH

JUAN PONCE DE LEÓN

Florida, 1521

Taínos, Africans,
gold, silver, copper—these people
are now thoroughly conquered, so I sail,
while others around me claim
that I plan my new voyage
only in search of magical waters,
a mysterious
fountain of youth . . .

even though my own truth
is so much simpler, just this ravenous
craving
for shiny minerals,
the glistening metals
of wealth.

IMAGINARY WEALTH

ESTEBANICO DE DORANTES

Texas, 1539

A dying explorer, I murmur news
of the wonders I've seen in this northern desert—
or wonders merely imagined—for how
can the feverish mind separate truth
from wishes?

Cíbola, city of turquoise and precious metals,
sparkling
in the distance . . .

For centuries after my death
surely every invader will seek
this fanciful land that I describe
so easily, allowing my name to live on
in glowing legends,
if not in the solid gold
of life.

POWER

JUAN DE OÑATE

New Mexico, 1598

I was born in New Spain, not Europe.
My family owns a silver mine in Zacatecas.
My wife is the granddaughter of Hernán Cortés,
who conquered the Aztec emperor Moctezuma—
but my wife is also the great-granddaughter
of that same defeated native emperor.
She's a mixed-race *mestiza*, child of two enemies,
such a fitting origin
for the mother of soldiers.

When King Felipe II of Spain orders me to claim
all the lands north of the Río Grande, I ride my horse
across a wide, shallow river, hoping for the riches
of Cíbola, where natives are said to dress themselves
in emeralds and gold.

Imagine my dismay
when all I find are ordinary towns,
small pueblos lit by the golden sun, surrounded
by cornfields
and bean vines.

•

My disappointed men threaten mutiny,
so I keep them marching farther and farther,
determined to be remembered
as the founder of cities—El Paso
and Santa Fe.

My legacy of strength will be built
atop ancient villages filled with the farms
and bones
of conquered tribes.

My wife calls me brutal
and greedy.

VICIOUS

VICENTE DE ZALDÍVAR

New Mexico, 1598

As Juan de Oñate's nephew, I march
to avenge the death of my brother
who was killed by villagers
while trying to conquer them.
The Acoma leader Zutacapán
knows our weakness, this need
for food, as we demand corn, beans,
squash, and then more corn—the true gold
of hungry soldiers.
Fire.
Blood.
I seize Acoma and chop off the feet
of twenty-four men, in order to set a horrifying
example for the others. Yes, Oñate's violence
is like a fever, contagious, destroying
everything in its path, including
my conscience.

WOMEN WHO WISH FOR PEACE

MARTA

New Mexico, 1598

Such cruelty!
Just like Juan de Oñate's wife, *yo soy una mestiza*, with mixed blood,
from a town near Mexico City. Yes, I'm part *india*,
but my sons are now expected to kill other *indios*,
these tribes of the north, here in quiet *pueblos*
that remind me so much of my own serene village
far to the south.

We call this journey our Dead Man's March,
because the desert's raging hunger
and endless thirst
almost
destroy us.

STORMING NORTHWARD

JUSEPE GUTIÉRREZ

Kansas, 1601

Oñate is never satisfied.
He already conquered the *pueblos*, but now
he craves these grasslands, wild prairies
with vast herds of massive creatures,
huge bison that assure us we are no longer
just seekers of treasure.
We need meat,
but while we hunt,
hidden hunters watch us and learn
how to master our powerful
horsemanship skills.

All it takes is a few runaway mares
to change everything forever, making Osage men
swifter than us and more skilled at riding
bareback.

CHOOSING SIDES

DOMINGO

New Mexico, 1680

Some of us—*mestizos* from villages
far to the south—join a rebellion,
fighting on the side of the brave people
of *los pueblos*, instead of supporting
wealthy noblemen who treat us
like beasts of burden.

With new hope for life as free men
instead of servants, we help send Spain's army
fleeing back across the same desert
they thought they'd conquered
so completely
long ago.

Choosing sides is not too difficult
when my only possibilities are misery
or hope.

RECONQUEST

DIEGO DE VARGAS

New Mexico, 1692

Drought begins to defeat the victorious rebels
of the *pueblos*, but only after they've been free
for a dozen years.
Crops need water.
People need food.
By the time my heavily armed troops
surround Santa Fe, I'm able to use bloodshed to force
acceptance of a treaty, but everything else
lingers beyond my control.

I can make the people of Acoma agree to pretend
that they are loyal subjects of Spain's king
and church, but there's no way to really know
secret feelings
hidden traditions
private beliefs.

HOMESICK

PEDRITO

Florida, 1702

Invasions, conquests, settlements,
then attacks by Englishmen and the French,
now rebellions by the Seminole, who try to reclaim
their ancestral land.

All I want is a chance to go home to my own *isla,*
my birthplace, the beautiful island called Cuba—but
if I had stayed there, I would still be a slave, merely
because of my Yoruba ancestry.
Volunteering as a soldier is the only
path to freedom
for a Cuban of African ancestry.

So I try to forget my family, and I struggle to dream
only of survival, here in the ragged town of San Agustín,
where Spain has already spent seven million *pesos*
trying to keep this troubled colony obedient.

TRADED

EDUARDO

Florida, 1763

England seized Cuba,
then traded it for Florida.

Now I'm suddenly expected
to be British.

Trading territories
means exchanging
one language
for another.

Will it be possible
for me to dream
without my own
familiar words?

FARM DREAMS

FRANCISCO

Louisiana, 1763

Fields
of
our
own
someday.
Cotton and sugarcane.
Fertile soil.

Spain received this region as the result of a peace treaty
with France and England. Now my parents endure hunger,
    disease, steamy heat,
saying it will all be worthwhile, if only I can become
a landowner—eventually,
instead of a blacksmith's
young apprentice, always wearing myself out,
bending my aching back
to shape glowing iron
into horseshoes and swords
for future battles.

IMAGINING LIBERTY

PABLO

Virginia, 1779

George Washington cannot win his war
for independence from England
without the help of Germans, Frenchmen,
and soldiers like me, young volunteers from all
the colonies of Spain.

Here on the cold snow of Yorktown,
I remember how it felt to be home in Venezuela's heat
when recruiters came, urging me to join a struggle
for the freedom
of northerners.

Now I secretly know that if I survive this battle,
someday I will be a rebel, too, ready to free
my own nation
from Spanish rule.

MISSION LANDS
CANDELARIA
California, 1779

We're expected to send money
to help George Washington, even though we
barely have enough to feed ourselves.

We came to this remote colony from Sonora,
leaving our Yaqui grandparents, pretending
we're not part *indio*—certain priests are willing
to help us change our origins on paper,
so that we will appear to be nearly pure Spanish,
the only settlers entitled
to own land.

Sheep, horses, cows—we have our reward,
but orchards and fields belong to la Misión de San Diego,
where the laborers are captured Kumeyaay, enslaved
without any choice.

HYPOCRISY

PADRE JUNÍPERO SERRA

California, 1784

I journeyed to *las Américas* after reading
the testimony of María de Jesús de Agreda,
a nun who described visiting *los indios*
by flying back and forth on the wings of angels.
I never imagined the military force I would need
to keep dozens of tribes obediently working
our mission fields, under the watchful eyes
of marching soldiers.

Sometimes I whip the captives myself.
Priests are expected to be gentle,
but without violence, Spain's *misiones*
in Alta California would be abandoned
by enslaved people who call me a monster
demonic.

THE ORPHAN PROJECT
APOLINARIA LORENZANA

California, 1800

I am the youngest
of twenty-one orphans
sent to Alta California
from Mexico City
to be given away
like puppies.

All our lives, we've lived
as sisters and brothers,
but now we're suddenly separated,
older girls handed out as wives,
and young ones like me given
as housemaids, while boys
go to mission soldiers
to serve as ranch hands
on the land they receive
in exchange for enslaving
los indios
of many tribes.

•

Fearfully, quietly, I learn
how to sew and cook the way priests demand,
and nurse the sick,
read a little bit,
and fashion pretty flowers
from scraps of smooth cloth.

There should always be
at least one beautiful
silk blossom
in each
lonely
orphan's
tragic
life.

HEALER

JUANA BRIONES

California, 1812

How can liberty mean so many
different things to various people?
My father is part *africano*, with ancestors
who were enslaved far to the south, in New Spain,
and my mother is part Yaqui, just like most
of the other settlers who came north from Sonora.

I'm only ten, but already I understand the shouts
of horsemen who gallop past our home at la Misión
de Santa Cruz—cries of *¡California libre!*
Free California!

But I can't worry about the independence hopes
of men. I have my chores—milking cows and learning
from Mamá and the captive Ohlone women
who show me how to cure wounds and fevers
with medicinal plants, nature's magic.

PACIFIC OCEAN

ARIZONA MISSION

Alaska

Hawaii

PART THREE

INDEPENDENCE FOR SOME

W N E S

Puerto Rico

ATLANTIC
OCEAN

NEWLY INDEPENDENT COUNTRIES

The people of Mexico and South America rose up against Spain's colonial empire, gaining independence. By now, most of the people of the region we refer to as Latin America were *mestizos*, a mixture of Indigenous, African, and Spanish ancestry.

In these new republics, enslaved Africans were freed. Only Puerto Rico and other Spanish colonies in the Caribbean had not yet gained independence and the abolition of slavery.

Despite the oppression and suffering brought by colonization, ordinary people struggled to remain strong and hopeful.

WONDERING ABOUT THE FUTURE

APOLINARIA LORENZANA

California, 1822

We suddenly belong to a newly
independent country
called Mexico.

There's already talk of closing the missions
and sending Spanish priests
back to their homeland,
leaving those of us
who depend
on these farmlands
abandoned.

So, while I worry and try to be hopeful,
I also continue folding cloth to make blossoms
of rippled petals with fancy edges
that are just as lovely
as wishes.

RIVERS ARE BORDERS

TERESITA
Wyoming, 1822

Quilts.
Beautiful patches.
Warmth.
The strength
of stitches.
Threads.
My skillful
hands.

Here on the northern border
of Mexico, my daughters and I
keep ourselves comforted by telling stories
about summer, while hoping my husband and sons
stay safe, never crossing the Yellowstone River
north into dangerous territory
ruled by foreigners.

INTRUDERS

MARTÍN DE LEÓN

Texas, 1824

I file my application for permission
to bring colonists to the Guadalupe Valley.
Relatives, friends, I wish we were enough—
but I need more settlers, so we decide to accept
Irishmen, and before I can stop them, more and more
foreigners from the United States
keep arriving
uninvited.

They have no papers,
no proper documents!

They behave as if they belong in Mexico,
even though we clearly know
they don't.

LAWBREAKERS

JOSÉ SÁNCHEZ

Texas, 1829

While surveying land, I notice
all the foreign squatters, who bring
their own ways with them,
including
slavery.

Men, women, children, all are forced to work
in fiercely hot, dusty, miserable
cotton fields.

Don't those lawbreakers from the US know
that enslaving people is now illegal in Mexico?

It's one of the reasons we overthrew
colonial Spain, to create a nation
of free men.

RANCH LANDS

TEODORO

Arizona, 1831

With Mexico City's government
so far away, missions close,
gardens and orchards wither,
tame cattle and horses
run wild.

Every ranch hand
claims what he can,
roping cows
and branding mustangs,
then hoping for rain
to keep the grass growing
so that animals and people
can survive.

PACIFIC OCEAN

LA PURÍSIMA CONCEPCIÓN

Alaska

Hawaii

PART FOUR
HEROES

Puerto Rico

ATLANTIC
OCEAN

FIGHTING FOR FREEDOM

The United States invaded Mexico, seizing land and persecuting millions of people who had gained, and soon lost, their independence. Meanwhile, Puerto Rico and the Caribbean island colonies of Spain were still fighting for freedom.

Throughout all these struggles, courageous individuals achieved amazing accomplishments in every aspect of life. Even when the obstacles seemed overwhelming, perseverance helped people face an uncertain future.

TRANSFORMED

JUANA BRIONES

California, 1851

Once again, my citizenship changes.
Española, mexicana, and now *norteamericana.*

A few years ago, the sudden invasion of gold miners
was quickly followed by the United States army,
and now I've been forced to flee my dairy farm
in San Francisco, just to keep my family safe
from roaming gangs that attack anyone
who speaks
Spanish.

I feel as if my tongue has been amputated,
but I won't let them change me too much.
When they seize my land, I make up my mind
to learn how to fight for my rights in court,
claiming English words
as my own.

BETRAYED

JUAN SEGUÍN

Texas, 1856

Born Texan, I fight for independence
from Mexico, hoping to create a free nation.
I fight at the Alamo, side by side with Americans,
and after we win, I'm elected senator, but then
I'm accused of treason, merely because my dark skin
makes pale men think of me
as an outsider.

Driven across the southern border,
I'm forced to choose between prison
and the Mexican army. How unfair it feels
to be compelled to fight this way, raiding
my beloved Texas
and living in a no-man's-land
between nations.

HIRED AND FIRED

SATURNINO

Kansas, 1860

We're valued as cowboys
all over the Great Plains.
My experience working cattle
at home on the Gran Chaco of Paraguay
helps these American ranchers forget
how proud I am of my own Guaraní
indio ancestry.

All this swift slaughter up here in the north
disturbs me so much that I argue with my boss
about killing wild bison, just to starve the Arapaho,
and then I have to ride away and search
for a city job
at a horse-racing stable.

Maybe I'll gradually adapt to sleeping
indoors.

EXILES

EMILIA CASANOVA

New York, 1863

Cubans and Puerto Ricans, all of us gather
in Brooklyn, or on West 29th Street, to speak
of rising up against Spain and uniting
in the struggle
for women's
suffrage—our right
to vote!

Meanwhile, our young men go willingly
into the United States army, fighting
on the side of the Union,
uniting
against slavery.

SONGBIRD

TERESA CARREÑO
Washington, DC, 1863

We came to this country from Venezuela
to escape a revolution, but now a civil war
rages all around me
as I walk into the White House
at President Lincoln's request.

He wants me to play a concert for his family
because he heard that I am called the Piano Girl.

I'm only ten years old, but performing
for Abraham Lincoln
helps me feel
winged.

SHOUTING!

RAMÓN EMETERIO BETANCES
New York, 1869

As a doctor, I'm dedicated to the battle
against cholera on my home island
of Puerto Rico, but I'm also determined
to end Spain's cruel colonial rule,
which still
allows slavery.

So I'm exiled, forced to flee, and now I live here
in New York City, where the success of the abolitionist cause
in this country gives me renewed strength to shout, protesting
injustice on the islands, keeping the plight
of enslaved people
in my heart.

EXCLUDED

PABLO DE LA GUERRA

California, 1870

Even though I've held many public offices,
now I'm eliminated from elections on the basis
of race.

So I hire a lawyer who proves my US citizenship,
but he can't convince the courts that I look
"white enough" to vote, run for office, or even
own land.

My proud brown skin color from *indios*
in my Mexican ancestry
will determine my future—a voiceless life
in this atmosphere of governmental
arrogance, unless the laws
are changed, and then
enforced.

LANGUAGE

LUISA

Colorado, 1870

I was born here, as were my parents,
and their parents, on and on for centuries.
Some of my ancestors were *mexicanos,*
others Cheyenne and Ute.

Now, suddenly, a man named Fred Walsen moves
into our little town, builds a brick house, and starts
to complain, saying no one in the town of Los Leones
should think of this place as anything other
than Walsenburg.

So we call him *el Fred.*
Doesn't he realize that English
is the newcomer
in our Spanish-speaking
tierra/land?

A LEADER

FERNANDITO

New York, 1880

Our grown-up neighbor is José Martí,
a man Papi admires for writing poetry.

He's a teacher, too, and a friend,
when he walks with us in Central Park,
teaching us the names of trees and flowers.

The poet tells us tales of elephants
and other wondrous creatures!
He encourages us to write our own stories
and verses, about anything that strikes us
as marvelous.

Someday, he promises, we'll all go back
to the island where we were born—someday,
when Cuba finally gains independence from Spain,
and *los esclavos* are set free—just like enslaved people
here in the US.

•

Someday, our island's future
will be as powerful
as an elephant,
because souls, the poet
assures us, have no color,
and shared hopes can rise up
to soar across any ocean
or border.

RANGE WARS

FÉLIX

New Mexico, 1890

We wear white hats, white capes, white masks,
as we ride through the night, cutting
barbed-wire fences.

We're careful never to hurt anyone.
All we want is open pasture for our livestock,
because we were here long before these new
fence-loving ranchers arrived.

Maybe we'll switch to elections as a path
toward preserving our traditional way of life.
How many local voters would support us
if we ran for seats in the Territorial Legislature?

Nearly all! We win!
Now we can show our faces in daylight,
unmasked!

CHANGING THE WORLD WITH WORDS

FERNANDITO

New York, 1898

Three years ago,
the sad news arrived
about José Martí's death
on a jungle battlefield in Cuba,
fighting for independence
from Spain.

So now, when I learn that the island's war
has ended with a horrifying betrayal
by the US—seizure not only of Cuba,
but of Puerto Rico, too—I remember
everything the brave poet taught me
about liberty, and I start to write
poetry of my own,
verses that protest
my adopted country's
policy of expansion—always
grabbing land, and more land—as if all the many
nations of North, Central, and South America
as well as the Caribbean islands

are meant to be possessions
of the US, instead of independent
countries.

In the shadow
of the Statue of Liberty,
I write about freedom
for everyone,
not just
us.

SO CLOSE

CATALINA
Puerto Rico, 1898

Spain had just granted
our independence
when the US
claimed our island
as their territory.

We were almost free!
Now what will happen
to our children,
our future?

STRIKE

DELANO GRAPE STRIKERS

SOLIDARI FOREV

PACIFIC OCEAN

¡CUIDADO!

Alaska

Hawaii

PART FIVE

¡SÍ SE PUEDE!

YES, WE CAN!

Puerto Rico

ATLANTIC
OCEAN

N

W   E

S

FIGHTING FOR JUSTICE AND INCLUSION

The twentieth century brought complex problems that were faced with ingenuity.

Education, work, economic mobility, legal rights, identity, and discrimination—there were many challenges and questions to be answered.

Empathy and compassion fueled powerful social justice movements.

DANGEROUS WORK

SANTIAGO

Montana, 1900

When I visit my family in Mexico,
neighbors hear that I earn three dollars each day
in dark mines, instead of a few cents in sunny fields.

After I return to my job in the north, a cousin
tries to follow, but he walks across the border
at the wrong time of year, reaching this frozen land
in winter, his feet forever damaged.

Soon, my children back home will be educated,
all because of my sacrifice in this deep,
crumbling tunnel
filled
with
poisonous
fumes.

SO MANY STRANGE FORMS
OF DISCRIMINATION

EUGENIO

Arizona, 1904

The courts won't let me serve on a jury,
just because my surname is Spanish—
but I have my own ideas
about justice.

When a mob raided the orphanage in Clifton,
they attacked nuns and kidnapped children.
The judge ruled that those rioters were just good
citizens, trying to rescue little ones
from the influence of Mexicans.

I don't see any other way to combat hatred,
so I plan to enroll in law school, even if it means
moving far away and coming back later
with my own powerful form
of influence.

REJECTED

ISABEL GONZÁLEZ

New York, 1904

Detained at Ellis Island. Questioned
in full view of the Statue of Liberty.
Classified as unacceptable! Denied entry.

When the United States seized Puerto Rico
and changed our island's name to Porto Rico,
we became dependents, but now I'm not allowed
on the mainland, even though my fiancé works here,
and we will soon be married, with a baby.

My court case is the first to ask: Are *puertorriqueños*
true Americans, or complete foreigners?
Will my child be a US citizen, or an outcast?
The legal decision is confusing. A new name for us
is invented. We are "noncitizen nationals" now,
neither equals
nor free.

ACTIVISM

JOVITA IDÁR

Texas, 1913

Born in Laredo, I witnessed
two lynchings.

Nothing else is the same after you've seen
people hanged for no other reason
than Mexican ancestry.

I became a teacher and a journalist,
writing about the brutality
of Texas Rangers who call themselves
law enforcement, while behaving
like criminals.

Women—educate yourselves!
Men—unite with us to demand justice!
As the first president of the League
of Mexican Women,
I concentrate on trying to provide
the treasure of education for poor children . . .

•

but my articles about US policies
toward Mexico
infuriate certain Texas Rangers.

When they come to my house
to destroy my printing press,
I stand in the doorway,
refusing
to move.

I already have a new plan—free
kindergarten
for the children
of poor families.

MIS PALABRAS/MY WORDS

LAURA

Puerto Rico, 1909

I'm a teacher who has suddenly been informed
that it's unacceptable to speak Spanish in our schools
on our own ancestral
    isla.
I have no choice but to tell the children about this new
    regla.
US rules can change anything they want,
even the island's official language, but laws
and hearts
are two different things.

At home, everyone continues to speak
and write with
    independencia.

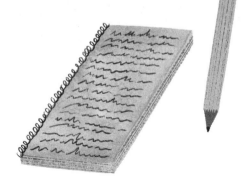

THE TRIUMPH OF CHILDREN!

LAURA

Puerto Rico, 1915

¡Los niños son heroes! Children are heroes!
They grew so angry about receiving
poor report cards that instead of switching
to English, they refused to attend school at all,
and now the rule has been changed, with classes
once again conducted in our own *español.*

Los niños chiquitos, only six or seven years old,
succeeded where teachers and parents failed!

Today, I feel like a student
who has finally
learned
a lesson.

DREAMS OF EQUALITY
ON THE BALL FIELD

JOSÉ MÉNDEZ

Missouri, 1916

In Cuba, I was called *el diamante negro,*
the black diamond—but here, my skin color
prevents me from playing in any major league,
so I pitch for the Kansas City All Nations,
a racially mixed team of blacks, whites,
American Indians, Hawaiians, Japanese,
and Cubans
like me.

Everyone says I'm one of this country's
best pitchers, and that if things were fair,
I'd make a lot of money, but instead
I'm trapped
in a system
that doesn't
make sense,
so I pitch
wherever I can,
letting the strength
of my arm
prove my worth.

TWO HOMELANDS

RAFAEL HERNÁNDEZ

New York, 1917

The law about Puerto Rican citizenship
finally changes, but only because
we are needed
as soldiers.

A strange new status
for *puertorriqueños*
won't let me vote
but causes me to be drafted
into the Harlem Hellfighters regiment
as a musician, playing to motivate troops
during a horror that so many people call
the Great War
only because it's huge,
certainly not because it's worthy
of so many deaths.

"Lamento borincano," my most famous song,
begins to write itself inside my heart
long before I endure the snowy northern winters
of my peaceful life
here at home

in New York,
so far
from my warm
tropical first home.
Tan lejos.
So distant.

THE GREAT MIGRATION

IGNACIO

Texas, 1918

Terrorized by the wild violence
of a long, desperate revolution in Mexico,
we flee our little village in Jalisco,
leaving all dreams of a normal life
far behind as we cross the vast desert,
perched on top of a dusty train
that overflows with refugees.

When we walk across the bridge
between Ciudad Juárez and El Paso,
we are just one small family
lost in a river of hunger
and wishes.

I never thought my proud mother
would beg, but what choice does she have?
Seeing her dirty, starving, and tearful,
I promise myself that never again
will anyone in my family
starve.

•

We are hard workers!
I'm only twelve, but that is old enough
to follow the harvest, plucking red tomatoes
from twining green vines
that smell
like hope-filled
growth.

FAMILY BRANCHES

PATRICIA
California, 1925

In the Central Valley, we all intermarry,
every farm laborer bringing originality
to his growing family tree—*mexicanos,*
filipinos, chinos, Bengalis . . .

With my Sikh father and half-Japanese, half-
Mexican mother, I'm just as American
as this farm's owner, because he's
half Swedish Armenian and half
German Russian.

Every year at the Fresno County Fair,
people dance in such varied styles
that the swirls of music
sound like a breeze
in a huge forest
with many leaves.

OUT OF THE SPOTLIGHT

ALFREDO CARLOS BIRABÉN

California, 1931

When I fell in love with the movies,
I left my home in Argentina and arrived
here in Hollywood, eager to play
any challenging role,
but the film studio
changed my name
to Barry Norton,
urging me to pretend
that I am not
myself.

While movies were silent,
I felt successful, but now
that sound has been added,
my accent prevents me
from being offered
good roles.

So while someone else plays Dracula by day
in a famous English-language version
of the film, I have to wait for night,

the only time when Spanish-speaking
movie crews are allowed to use
the studio.

Any role I play will be powerful,
because
of my authentic
anger.

THE GREAT DEPRESSION

EMILIA CASTAÑEDA

California, 1933

Papi has worked in Los Angeles
for so many years that you would think
he'd be appreciated for his experience
and skill, but instead, just as soon as the economy
weakens and millions of people need work,
my father is suddenly thought of as a thief
who steals some other American's job.

Will we really be deported?
My brother Francisco and I were born here,
and at school we speak English . . .

but now we are informed that if we want to stay
in the United States, we must declare ourselves
to be orphans with no living parents, so that we
can be placed in an orphanage, given away
to strangers. When we refuse to deny
that our father is alive,
we're shoved into a noisy crowd
of other helpless children
at the train station,

all of us forced to travel south
with our parents, going "back"
to Mexico, a country we've
never
even
seen.

Why are we being punished?
Our families have never committed
any crime!

WORDS OF PROTEST

ISABEL GONZÁLEZ

New Jersey, 1935

After the court case
that denied my citizenship
back at the turn of the century,
I decided to fight for the rights
of *puertorriqueños*
with heartfelt letters
to the *New York Times,*
writing over and over,
always defending justice,
with words as my only weapons.
Now, when I open the newspaper to read
my own protests, I see shocking articles
about events in California, where children
born American are being deported to Mexico.
What does it take to be fully accepted?
We know the truth—we belong here.
We're citizens.

A FAMOUS ARTIST

PATROCIÑO BARELA

New Mexico, 1936

As a child, I had to work hard, wandering
from state to state, taking jobs on farms
and in mines, mills, rail yards.

I never learned to read or write,
but my hands know how to carve
wild juniper wood
into statues
of *santos*—saints.

Time magazine calls me the discovery
of the year, because I am the first artist
of Hispanic ancestry
to have my work shown
at the Museum of Modern Art
in New York, even though my statues
are an ancient style,
not modern,
and all I ever
intended to do
was stay up late

finishing two arms
and hands, leaving
the dream
of a face
for the next
morning.

SMOKE

DOLORES

California, 1937

On cold winter nights
when a hard frost threatens to destroy
the orange crop,
orchard foremen bang on our doors
to wake us up
and make us go out to light flames
in smudge pots
surrounded by darkness.

We pour oil into the pots,
hoping to keep the air warm enough
to save the lives of treasured trees,
our only source
of jobs.

My lungs
fill with soot
that makes me cough,
and while I'm gasping,
my smoke-blackened skirt
catches fire!

Now, from this hospital window,
I can see a billboard that shows
smiling blond ladies
in flowered dresses,
wearing clean straw hats
as they perch on tidy ladders
to pluck ripe oranges
and place them in quaint
baskets.

Do city people who shop
in neatly organized grocery stores
actually believe that the fiery lives
of real farmworkers
don't exist?

AIRBORNE

MANUEL GONZÁLEZ

Hawaii, 1941

I'm a fighter pilot from Texas,
but rude strangers keep calling me
"the Mexican," instead of using my name
and my rank: ensign.

I don't even care too much
once I'm up here in mid-sky
hoping these Pearl Harbor
bombs
don't strike
too close,
catching my plane
in the crossfire
so that I'll fall
into the ocean
a sacrifice,
nameless.

SEGREGATED

EUGENE CALDERÓN

Alabama, 1942

No one knows how to classify
an East Harlem Puerto Rican
gang leader.

In the white officers' barracks,
everyone complains that I'm too dark,
but in the black officers' barracks,
they tell me I'm too light,
so the Tuskegee Airmen
end up inventing
a third barrack,
just for me
and one other
Latino.

Then they start moving me
from state to state,
all over this cold,
snowy country,
just to keep me
from gaining

enough
training hours
to fly . . .

but I know the meaning
of the word perseverance.
I'll never give up, so they won't
defeat me!

MEDICINE

HÉCTOR GARCÍA

Texas, 1942

I'm a doctor, so I should be
a medical officer,
but recruiters send me
to the infantry,
refusing to believe
that someone born
in another country
could ever be so educated,
even though my parents
were both teachers
before they were forced
to flee the violent revolution
in Mexico
many years ago.

So now I fight two wars,
this armed one against enemies
of my beloved United States,
and a quiet, personal struggle
against racism, fought just by proving
my dedication

to healing wounds
and saving lives
with equal concern
for all.

ZOOT SUIT

RAMÓN

California, 1943

All we wanted to do was dance
the jitterbug, like everyone else.

Twelve years old, stripped of my clothes,
attacked, beaten, humiliated, simply because
my jacket and slacks are a new style, loose, cool.

When the police finally arrive,
they just laugh and praise
all those racist sailors
for raging against
the color of skin
beneath
clothes.

Is there any way in the world
that I'll ever understand hatred?
Why do all the newspapermen
who take my picture
write about Zoot Suit Riots
instead of giving their articles

more truthful titles
like Sailor Rage?

Why have we
been arrested,
instead of them?

This is wartime!
Shouldn't those US Navy men
find real enemies to attack
instead of ordinary
neighborhood kids
like me and my
friends?

GUEST WORKERS

CARMEN

California, 1944

With so many men away at war,
once again, *mexicanos* are welcomed
to the north as laborers, recruited
by big companies and the US government,
invited to work on farms and in factories,
building airplanes.

They call me Rosita the Riveter,
ignoring
my real name.

I sweat side by side with white and black
women, all of us strong, hardworking, brave.
Just watch us; we're strong women; we won't
go back to being silent, not after this.

BUS RIDE

ARMANDO SÁNCHEZ

Florida, 1945

I'm a drummer for a band.
I'm tired, so I sit in the middle
of the bus, not the back.

When someone tells me to move,
I refuse.

So what if I'm dark skinned,
and Cuban?

I'm American, too, with the right
to sit freely.

So I keep that seat
all the way to New York.
Sometimes staying in one place
is what it takes to move forward.

WAR HERO

MACARIO GARCÍA

Texas, 1947

I landed at Normandy, fought my way across France,
survived explosions in Belgium, destroyed
whole machine-gun nests, and charged
a dangerous hill to protect my buddies.

Bronze Star.
Purple Heart.
Medal of Honor.

Not even the way newspapers praise my courage,
calling me the Fearless Mexican—not even that
was enough to make a restaurant owner back home
in Texas
serve me a meal
two years ago, when I stepped through a door
that had a sign warning:
NO DOGS, NO MEXICANS.

I entered anyway,
determined to prove
that I have rights,
but when a fight started,

I was the only one
who ended up
in jail.

It's going to take a few more years
of courageous protests before all people
from every background can enjoy the freedom
we fought for
when we were
heroes
overseas.

THE COURAGE TO DANCE

JOSÉ LIMÓN

New York, 1947

After serving in the US Army,
I return
to my own
natural world,
the stage!

So many people say that ballet
and modern dance
are too feminine for men,
but I crave wings,
so I soar
inside the theater,
proving that strong muscles
can help me become
an eagle.

Human movement is a bridge
between solid ground
and dreamlike air.

•

Leap, fall, rise!
Work, listen, learn!

At school in Tucson, Arizona,
other children made fun of my accent,
so I studied constantly, mastering
the pronunciation of each English syllable
perfectly.

Now I work just as hard at teaching
young dancers how to fly
like the songbirds I watched
in my grandmother's garden
back in Mexico, long before
I became
my winged
self.

BRACERO

EMILIO

California, 1948

Millions of laborers from Mexico
are recruited by the US, to use
our strong *brazos*—our arms—
for farm work.

My first home in this rich
northern nation
is a chicken coop.

I promise myself it won't be my last home,
because I plan to work hard, sending money
back to my family and saving whatever I can,
making sure my children will be able to stay in school
instead of bending
over strawberry plants,
sweating so that someone else enjoys
a sweet dessert.

PLANS FOR THE FUTURE

HÉCTOR GARCÍA

Texas, 1949

As a doctor, I managed
to become respected
after the war,
but when I see
how other veterans
are treated, it makes me so angry,
especially when funeral homes
refuse to bury the remains of men
like Félix Longoria—a war hero
who died in battle, his bones
finally
delivered
to his family
after four years
of peace.

My anger gradually
turns into a plan: I'll fight back
against unfairness, but not with weapons,
just words.

•

I'll organize a civil rights movement
for soldiers, and another for farmworkers,
and a third to defend
voting rights.

No politician
will dare to ignore us
when we unite at the polls!

BORDER CROSSING

JUAN

California, 1950

I walk
all night

jump fences

outrun dogs

escape gunfire

end up
lost

then somehow discover
my own footsteps,
leading me back
to this path of weariness
under an avocado tree

where I sleep
in a bed of leaves
trembling
from this mixed-up sense

of loss and gain
that makes me yearn
to follow my papi
who left home

as a *bracero*

and never found
his way
back

to
me.

AN INDIVIDUAL

YMA SUMAC

New Jersey, 1953

Radio in the '40s,
then Capitol Records,
my South American folk songs,
half a million albums sold
so swiftly!

And now, this melody of forest creatures,
my rare, five-octave vocal range, a chance
to reveal the double voice, a talent
called eerie because, alone, I sound
like two people
singing together.

Low and warm.
High and birdlike.
Music critics praise my variations,
in between their endless descriptions
of my Peruvian childhood
as a direct descendant
of the Inca emperor Atahualpa.

•

I refuse to be remembered
only for my ancestry.

I insist that reporters acknowledge
my completely unique
voice.

HOLLYWOOD

JOSÉ FERRER

California, 1954

My family brought me to the mainland
from our island home in Puerto Rico
when I was only six.

I studied hard and was accepted
by Princeton at the age of fourteen—
but I didn't choose to start right away—first
I prepared at a school in Switzerland
for an extra year.

College at fifteen. Architecture. Jazz. Theater!
I experiment until I realize that I'm a natural actor,
capable of switching
back and forth
between Shakespeare plays
and light comedy,
all of it equally enjoyable.

As the first US Latino to win an Oscar,
I should be respected, but unlike so many others,
I never agree to change my name to an English one,

and I don't like to accept roles that mock my ancestry
with silly
stereotypes.

So now, when I'm asked by the FBI
to accuse my colleagues of being disloyal
to the United States government, I refuse.

Blacklisted in Hollywood, I leave for New York's
Broadway stage plays, where I feel right at home
transforming myself into Don Quixote,
the imaginative knight who strives to right
all the wrongs
of life's
complicated
reality.

EDUCATION CHANGES EVERYTHING

EUGENE CALDERÓN

New York, 1957

All that segregated unfairness
when I was a Tuskegee Airman
back in the war years
definitely
left its mark.

Instead of going back
to my East Harlem gang,
I went to college
and then graduate school,
and now I've returned
to my old turf
as a police officer,
recruiting other *puertorriqueños*
to defend the neighborhood—
el barrio—from violence.

Next, I plan to join
the Department of Education,
where I'll be an official,
recruiting Latino teachers

so that children will have a chance
to survive
and enjoy
an educated
future.

Maybe I'll even organize
a *museo del barrio*—our own
unique museum
for teaching history
through art!

PEDRO PAN

CRISTINA AND ELENA

Rhode Island, 1962

They call us the Peter Pan children
because we arrived alone, our parents
left behind
in Cuba.

The revolution on our island
is too complicated for us to understand.

We're only nine years old—twin sisters
with living parents who sent us to the US
as if we were orphans, because they thought
we would be safe here.

We've had to live in one foster home
after another, sometimes together, often
separate.

Miami was a little bit easier,
but Denver was just lonely snow,
and here all we can think of all winter
is when will Mami and Papi

finally
arrive?

What if they never
get permission
to leave
the isolated
island
at all?

EL CLUB CUBANO

VIVIANA

New Jersey, 1965

We lost our home, jobs, happiness,
and way of life
when we fled the island
as refugees
on Freedom Flights.

So we start clubs in Elizabeth and Union City,
where everyone gathers to remember and dream
of night stars gleaming on the serene waters
of *el Río Armendares* and *el Río Manatí*.

All week, we work as waitresses and janitors,
even though we used to be dentists and doctors
on the island.

Until we learn English,
weekends at the club
with songs and dances
will have to be enough
to keep us hopeful.

Music is the only part of home
that we were able to carry away
hidden deep inside
our rhythmically beating
hearts.

TRANSITION

AMALIA

New York, 1965

My family left the Dominican Republic
because of all the political trouble,
a situation so disturbing and tragic
that whenever grown-ups
talk about it,
they either whisper
or holler
at each other.

All I want now is peace at school,
where everyone separates into groups
from different countries, Spanish-speaking
or English, so that I'm always somewhere
in between.

EXILE OR IMMIGRANT?

CARIDAD

Florida, 1968

My parents brought me here
when I was a baby, almost ten years ago.

I don't remember Cuba, but I've seen
plenty of photographs, and I know
we call ourselves exiles, always dreaming
of going back . . .

but I wonder if it will be up to me to decide
when the time comes—should I stay
and become a United States citizen,
or move back to an island
that might no longer
feel
like my real
home?

¡HUELGA!

RAY

California, 1968

In the town of Delano, surrounded by vineyards,
my family can't afford to buy even one bunch
of grapes.

Our work on farms keeps other Americans
well fed, but we sleep in shacks or cars,
with no bathrooms, no water, not even
a river, just polluted irrigation canals.

I pick fruit all day, before and after school.
Scorching sun, hunger, thirst, discouragement.
Nothing ever changes, until *la huelga*—the strike!

It started three years ago, when Filipino workers
were the first to walk out, soon followed
by Mexican Americans like my parents,
who were born in California
but are still treated like foreigners.

All we ask for is minimum wage, but farmers
are used to paying migrants much less, so they

bring in strikebreakers from Mexico, people
who really need work and don't understand
what it's like
to be born here
yet so easily
replaced.

Next, another sort of strikebreaker appears.
Men in pickup trucks, swinging clubs and yelling
insults.

Our leaders, César Chávez and Dolores Huerta,
have taught us to be peaceful, following the examples
of Martin Luther King and Mohandas Gandhi, so now,
when brutal thugs attack us, we fall to our knees
and pray.

Nonviolence works slowly, but it does eventually
succeed in changing the minds of people in cities
who watch TV news and see how we're treated.

Eventually, ordinary shoppers join our grape boycott,
refusing to buy any fruit harvested by workers
who don't earn a decent wage.

•

Now the landowners don't have any choice.
To stay in business, they have to sign
labor contracts, proving that peace
can win against violence,
with fairness replacing
injustice!

VOTING RIGHTS

WILLIE VELÁSQUEZ

Texas, 1969

In towns like Crystal City, Mexican-Americans
live on one side and everyone else
on the other.

Teachers demand English, but some students
only know Spanish, and others prefer to blend
both or shift back and forth, like the natural flow
of a winding stream on the Rio Grande floodplain.

After kids hear about walkouts
at schools in California, they march out, too,
calling themselves Chicanos now, instead of
using a hyphen.

Those farmworker strikes
spread to our Texas fields, but when violence
enters the picture, people separate
into factions, argumentative groups
that believe this or that, when really
all we need

is unity
at the voting polls.

So that's my only goal now: voter registration
and making sure our votes count.
Millions of votes.
Millions.

ANTI-WAR

FRANK DEL OLMO

California, 1970

Rich boys avoid the military draft
by staying in college, but poor ones
die in Vietnam.

So many Mexican American soldiers
are sent to the violent front lines
that back here in Los Angeles,
families march, shout, and even
throw rocks
to protest.

Policemen attack.
My journalism mentor—Rubén Salazar—is shot
and killed. Can it be a coincidence?

I don't think so, because everyone knows
he's been documenting police brutality.

His death leaves the *Los Angeles Times*
without a journalist who can speak Spanish,
so I move into the essential role

of bilingual
investigative
reporter.

It's hard to believe that just a few years ago,
I tried to volunteer to be a fighter pilot.
It's lucky I had bad eyesight and was rejected
by the air force.

Otherwise, I never would have gone to college
and learned how to make up my own mind
about war and other
sorrows.

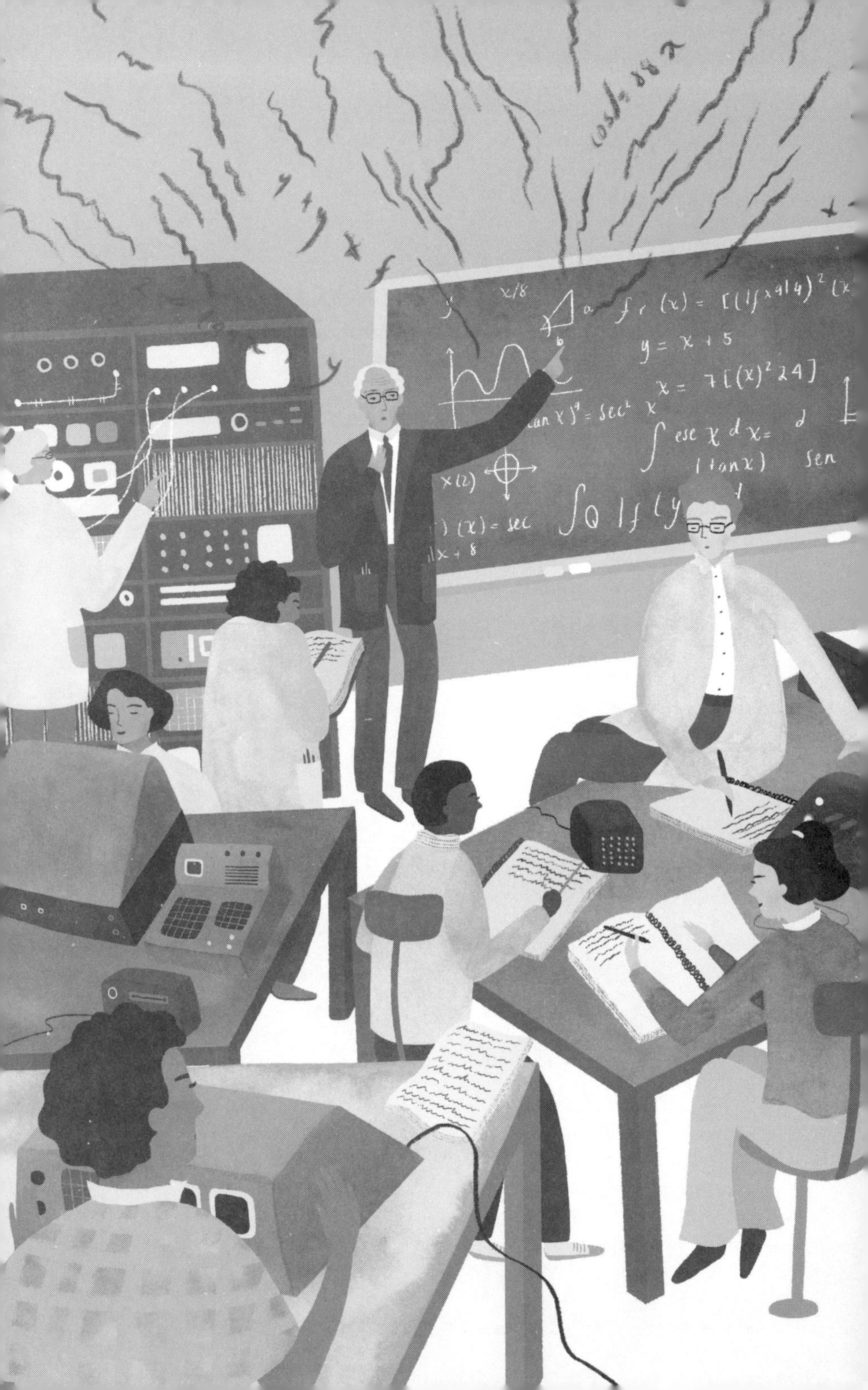
y = x + 5
sen

A MATHEMATICAL GENIUS

ALBERTO CALDERÓN

Illinois, 1974

As a child in Argentina, numbers already
amazed me, and when I grew older, I began
to realize that I could offer easier ways
to solve
complex problems
that even adults
could not
understand.

A scholarship brought me to Chicago,
where my engineering background
now helps me turn fascinating ideas
into useful ones.

Whenever I have a chance, I return
to my homeland, where I find talented students
and help them travel here to continue
their studies.

•

There's no end to the wide variety
of problems—both mathematical and social—
that can be solved simply by combining
education
and compassion.

RECRUITED BY A FACTORY

ALFONSO

Massachusetts, 1975

Businessmen came to the mountains
of Colombia, in search of weavers who know
how to string a loom
and create cloth.

When I left my home far behind,
I thought this textile mill in the cold north
would employ me forever, but now it's closing,
so I'll have to move my whole family
to North or South Carolina,
where there are rumors of jobs
weaving threads of cotton
into beautiful patterns,
or even just fixing
broken looms.

THREE LANGUAGES

MERCEDES

Illinois, 1980

When war broke out
and the death squads came,
we fled through Mexico,
leaving Guatemala
forever.

My husband was gone,
my babies so young,
and when the people
who smuggle refugees
made me work
as a maid in a hotel,
I never imagined that I
would be able to learn
a third language,
but here in Chicago,
my children already
know how to flow back and forth
between English and Spanish at school,
before returning to K'iche' Maya
at home, where I feel free

to wear my own
embroidered clothing,
instead of that stiff, ugly
toilet-cleaning
uniform.

BOATLIFT

ORESTES

Florida, 1980

We arrive by the thousands,
then tens of thousands, until we become
one hundred and twenty-five thousand total,
a sea
of desperate
refugees
floating
from the port
of Mariel
in Cuba.

Floating to our new homeland, where angry
grandchildren of refugees from Europe
complain
and insult us
because we speak Spanish.
Don't they know that we'll learn?

•

Refugee is such a simple word,
so similar to *refugiado*,
yet somehow
at the same time
refuge seems infinitely
complicated.

TEACHING

JAIME ESCALANTE

California, 1982

In my native Bolivia, the students were hungry,
but here in Los Angeles, students are also poor.

Poverty, I show them,
can be temporary.

In the past, I've had to work mopping floors
and washing dishes, but now I'm back
to my real passion, helping young people
qualify
for college.

FRAGMENTS

MARÍA
Washington, DC, 1985

When El Salvador grew too war-torn
for children, a church helped my parents
bring me and all my brothers and sisters
here, where *danger* is a word I see
all around me, at school,
every day.

Guns on the street
are just as perilous as guns
in battle.

Refugee and *asylum* now seem like words
caught between shattered fears
and flowing
hopes.

OPPORTUNITIES

ANGELES ALVARIÑO

California, 1987

Arrow worms, umbrella jellyfish, siphonophores.
I've spent my whole life studying these three
groups of creatures that dwell in deep oceans.

When I was a professor in Spain, I had no idea
that I would be offered a chance to work
in San Diego.

Now I've shown how certain jellyfish
are particularly sensitive to fluctuations
in water temperature.

Climate change?
Is such a thing possible?
If the trends I've noticed are true,
then we need to seize
every opportunity
to figure out why
the world's oceans
are growing warmer,

so that we can discover

scientific ways

to protect

nature.

ENGLISH-ALSO

MARTÍN

Arizona, 1988

I arrived in the US
stuffed under the hood
of a pickup truck.

From Nicaragua to Honduras,
then El Salvador and Guatemala,
always crossing
through a zigzag
of wartime
dangers.

By the time I reached Mexico, all I had left
was the air in my breath, and these
nightmares.

So I enroll in English classes just as soon
as I reach Tucson, because this is my life now,
and I don't think the state of Arizona
should have passed that unfair
English-only law
that doesn't make sense

to any parent who wants
smart children to quickly learn
two ways of being understood,
instead of only
one.

FIELD TRIP

GONZALO

California, 1994

Today our class visits a museum
where I see a quilt with a flowered border,
barbed wire,
and a ghostly,
nearly invisible
image of a family
running.

It looks just like the warning signs on roads
where Mami and I ran when we crossed
the border from Tijuana and then
had to race across busy freeways
in the United States, escaping
Border Patrol cars
that tried to chase us.

At the museum, I study a little square of paper
on the wall, a printed note that gives the name
of the quilt artist: Consuelo Jiménez Underwood,
a Mexican American of Huichol *indio* ancestry.

•

She grew up in a migrant farmworker family
like mine.

Does that mean that I, too,
could become an artist,
using my own
memories
from distant Oaxaca,
with pictures and words
from our Mixteca language,
to create visions of beauty
wrapped in barbed wire
bordered by flowers
of hope?

A SCIENTIFIC HERO

MIREYA

Massachusetts, 1995

The Massachusetts Institute of Technology.
Who could have guessed that I, a quiet, shy
immigrant from Uruguay, would ever
have the chance to learn from the same
earth, atmosphere, and planetary science
professor—Dr. Mario Molina—who won
the Nobel Prize!

Born in Mexico and educated in Europe,
he earned his doctorate in California,
where he researched the damaging effects
of certain chemicals used in air conditioners
and refrigerators, compounds that have now
been completely banned all over the world,
because the brilliant Dr. Molina proved
that they were destroying
our earth's
precious
atmosphere.

•

One scientist
can make
such a difference!

Imagine a whole team of minds, struggling
to understand climate change, so that we
can solve atmospheric problems
before it is too late
to correct
our careless
everyday
mistakes.

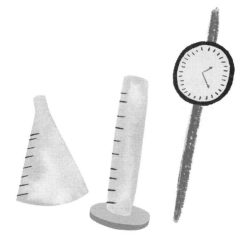

WE ARE NOT VILLAINS

ALFONSO WILLIAMSON

Connecticut, 1996

Born in New York, I spent much of my childhood
back in Colombia with my family, before returning
to the United States at the age of twelve,
when Flash Gordon comics gave me
visions of courage.

I knew I would be an artist someday.
Now I'm old, and I've already brought
the Star Wars movies into comic book form.
Daredevil, Spider-Man, Spider-Girl,
I've worked on them all . . .

but it will take more than a superhero
to bring peace, to end the drug wars
that pass back and forth like storms
raging across my family's
two countries.

FREEDOM FIGHTER

ROBERTO

Illinois, 1999

Out of prison.
Pardoned.
Nineteen and a half years of my life sacrificed.
Those bombs were futile—I see that now—
but the cause of independence for Puerto Rico
still seems right to me, because as long as we
remain a commonwealth instead of a country,
people like me will feel owned, like objects,
instead of included,
as equals.

A least that's how I feel, but my sister says she wants
statehood, and my brother claims he'd like everything
to just stay exactly the way it is.
Mixed up.

PACIFIC OCEAN

DREAMERS
ARE HERE
TO STAY

DEFEND
DACA

CAUTION!

¡CUIDADO!

CAUTION!

Alaska

Hawaii

PART SIX

FOR OUR LIVES

Puerto Rico

ATLANTIC
OCEAN

CURRENT TIMES

The twenty-first century has been so filled with turmoil that sometimes it's easy to forget the way vast rivers of hopeful dreams ripple and flow through this nation, along with all the troubling confusion.

Young people are learning how to become leaders. Young people are learning the skills they will need to vote wisely. Voting means power. Voting changes the future. Voting brings hope.

EMERGENCY RESPONSE

RAMÓN SUÁREZ

New York, 2001

We charge into the burning remnants
of crumbling towers. Trying to save lives,
we lose
our own.

Those who survive call us heroes, but we were
policemen, firefighters, and ambulance drivers
long before terrorists
attacked.

Now we float—yes, we soar
high above smoke and ash, knowing why
we chose our jobs, no matter how dangerous.

Survivors exist
because of us.

VOLUNTEERS

CECILIA

Virginia, 2004

We come from every state,
offering to sacrifice our own safety
so that others
will be safe.

Heroes?
Maybe.

After the loss of both legs,
my best friend goes home, but I'm
still overseas, wondering how long
these wars
will last . . .

Iraq.
Afghanistan.
Terrorism seems to be spreading.

•

We can't invade every country,
so maybe it's time for me to discover
some other way to fight for peace,
by helping the hungry
and building schools,
instead of by
shooting.

JUMPING HIGH

CONNIE

Georgia, 2004

This year's worldwide games
are so much fun to watch,
because my hurdle-leaping hero—
Félix Sánchez—is the winner
of the Dominican Republic's first
Olympic gold medal!

Even though he grew up in San Diego,
he has dual citizenship with the DR,
just like I do with Costa Rica.

Maybe someday when I'm older,
I'll be a famous athlete, too, running fast
and leaping sky high, crossing all sorts
of seemingly impossible barriers.

LEARNING FROM EACH OTHER

RIGOBERTO

Wisconsin, 2004

When the Panamanian art workshop teacher
speaks with shapes on paper,
I understand so easily.

Sometimes I'm homesick for Ecuador,
but at this unique school for the deaf,
Spanish sign language is different
from the English form,
and I am learning so much!

For me, the happiest way to communicate
is by studying Miss Irisme's
starry colors, and then letting my own world
of painted birds
and dancing trees
soar!

CONFUSED

BIENVENIDA

Michigan, 2006

My parents left Mexico
after big corporations
pushed small family farms out of business,
so they could no longer afford to grow corn
for a living.

Now Mamá and Papá are being deported.
I'll be here alone in my own birthplace,
a United States citizen trying to finish high school
without my parents
and my older sister, Matilde, who was born
across the border.

Will any of my loved ones ever be able
to return here, to my natural home?

DIVIDED

MATILDE

Arizona, 2006

I try to return to my little sister, Bienvenida,
in Detroit, but fences and rifles stop me.

Who are these men
armed like soldiers,
patrolling the border
as if my simple effort
to live in the place
where I grew up
were suddenly
an act
of war?

MARCHING

JOE

California, 2006

Nearly a million people march together,
some only waving American flags—others
with two banners to show equal pride
in dual origins.

Traffic stops. News crews film.
A camera focuses on my sign:
TODAY WE MARCH. TOMORROW WE VOTE.

No, I'm not undocumented, I explain to a reporter.
In fact, most of my ancestors lived right here
in Los Angeles long before it became part
of Mexico, but as a lawyer, I believe in fair laws
for everyone, and that includes children
whose parents have been
deported.

COUNTING

MARISOL

Alaska, 2010

When census officials come to the door,
Mamá pretends we're not home so she won't
have to answer nosy personal questions.

Months later, at school, I learn that this country
now includes fifty million people of Latino ancestry,
with more than 60 percent born on US soil.

I wonder how many there would be if no one
was afraid to be counted.

How would they figure me out anyway,
when my family is half Irish Australian
and half Peruvian Chinese?

IDENTITY

ANA

Arizona, 2010

As a police officer, I find it disturbing
to be ordered
to check all the official documents
of anyone
who merely *looks* Latino
like half of my own
mixed-together family.

But a new law requires interrogations,
so now, when I'm out of uniform, I know
how it feels to worry about being mistaken
for someone who happens to be
foreign born.

SUCCESS

LUIS

California, 2010

My grandparents brought me from Chile
in 1973, right after my parents disappeared,
victims of a brutal, US-supported dictatorship.
I've never figured out why so many refugees
choose the same country that caused us
to need refuge.

Now I'm a computer science professor,
living near Berkeley, where I enjoy seeing names
of other *chilenos* in the newspaper, especially
Matías Duarte, an inventor.

Freedom of the press and freedom of speech
are just as important to me
as understanding
the marvels of technology.

DREAMS OF CITIZENSHIP

HÉCTOR

Oregon, 2012

Finally, DACA is a way for families
to stay together, so that millions of us
who were brought to this country as children
might have a chance to seek legal status.

Maybe I won't have to give up my college classes . . .
but even if it works out so that no one can deport me,
what about my parents?
Do I really have to write down their names and tell
every detail about the way they came and how long
they've stayed?

Will this chance for me to dream
of a safe future for myself
turn into a nightmare
for them?

DREAMS OF BEAUTY

ROSARIO

California, 2014

So many years have passed
since my grandparents left Honduras
with nothing, and now finally we own
a greenhouse filled with glorious flowers.

All those decades of landscape labor,
raking leaves and fixing sprinklers,
finally gave us a way to make a living
by growing tropical orchids for weddings,
proms, and Mother's Day.

Tomorrow night at my *quinceañera*
all the bouquets will be special in a way
that brings past and future into full view,
a celebration of old
and young
working together.

FAMILY REUNION

NANCY

Washington, 2015

Translating for my grandma was fun
when I was little, but now that I'm twelve,
I just wish she would learn English
like everyone else in Seattle.

Abuela says it isn't easy,
shaping her mouth
into new sounds.

Does she know that this isn't easy for me, either,
always guessing what strangers are thinking
at the grocery store, post office, bank, and clinic?
At least there's a nurse who knows enough Spanish
to set me free
during school hours.

Next month, when we finally visit
all the cousins I've never met—in Cuba—
Abuela says she'll be the one interpreting
confusing words
for me.

•

I never thought I would see her so thrilled
with these new laws that suddenly renew
diplomatic relations and normal travel
between Abuela's birthplace
and mine,
after all those old
complicated
Cold War hostilities
that lasted more than half a century,
tearing whole families
apart.

ESL

LEONEL

Pennsylvania, 2015

In our English as a Second Language class,
Julia from Argentina and Marisol from Mexico
sit side by side, agreeing that English is not
our second language.

For Julia, it's her fourth, after Italian from her mother
and Spanish from her father, and Portuguese
from a year as an exchange student in Brazil.
For me, it's a third language, after the Creole
I picked up from my Haitian father
and Spanish from my mother
in the Dominican Republic.

Sometimes it's hard for me to imagine
knowing only one way of describing
hope.

DREAMS OF RAIN

ADRIANA

California, 2015

Nothing but dust
where endless vegetable fields
used to grow.

Unemployed laborers struggle to pay
for their lunches, here at Papi's restaurant,
where I help in the kitchen during summer vacation,
making *pupusas* so that Central Americans
will feel at home.

One more rainless winter will put us
out of business, just like my great-grandpa
in the last century, when farms without water
turned to dust, and instead of going back
to Mexico, he grew creative,
and started
experimenting
with recipes.

.

I'm already halfway through college,
and even though the rest will take hard work,
I'll manage, because sooner or later
there will surely be
rain clouds in the sky,
pouring out water
for rivers
of growth.

THE HORRORS OF HISTORY
ARE HAPPENING RIGHT NOW

GLORIA

New York, 2016

I don't understand why my teachers
keep speaking of things that are ancient,
when so many of the same old mistakes
are being repeated all over again—
racism, scapegoats, deportations.
The angry past is still alive, thriving
inside this monstrous
presidential candidate
who insults us.

The whole world needs bridges, not walls,
education, not nuclear weapons.

I don't care what anyone says.
I know what I think.
We need peace,
not hatred.

ABANDONED

SONIA

Puerto Rico, 2017

Hurricanes, one after another,
first Irma, then María, storms with names
that sound so harmless, even though
they leave us suffering, hungry, thirsty.
No electricity. No medicine.

When help finally arrives, it's just a fraction
of what is needed, as if the US government
still doesn't think of us as complete citizens.

We pay taxes, but we can't vote in national
elections—taxation without representation,
and now this ugly abandonment, so we help
each other, following the heroic example
of Carmen Yulín Cruz, the courageous mayor
of San Juan.

INJUSTICE

NANCY

Washington, 2018

Unfairness takes so many forms
that it's hard to keep up with the changes!

Cuba is being shunned again, by this new
US administration that seems to prefer
chaos
instead of order.

Why can't Congress lift
the trade embargo and travel restrictions,
treating a neighboring nation like a friend?

I'm young, but I have enough common sense
to know that peace
is always a worthwhile goal.

NEVER DREAMLESS

HÉCTOR

Oregon, 2018

DACA has ended.
We don't know our future.
We could all be deported.
I'm afraid, but I speak up.
I march, I protest,
I sing.

ENOUGH

ELSA

Florida, 2018

Emma González inspires me.
We had a shooter at our school, too.
I survived.

No more weapons of war on campus!
Enough is enough! We march for our lives.
When politicians won't defend us from killers,
we'll protect ourselves by voting them out.

Emma has brown skin and green eyes, just like mine.
I'm Puerto Rican, and she's Cuban American;
I'm straight, she's bi; I'm shy, she's bold; but we're both
equally brave
in our own ways,
because she speaks out loud,
while I shout on paper, ENOUGH IS ENOUGH,
let's VOTE, MARCH, SING, WRITE!

•

We have to be leaders, not followers,
so that we'll never again
be herded like sheep
toward a helpless
slaughter.

We are the hopeful future,
triumphing over this country's
troubled past.

ACKNOWLEDGMENTS

I thank God for dreams, my family for encouragement, many wise proofreaders for corrections and suggestions, Dr. Sandra Garza, Ydalmi Noriega, my agent Michelle Humphrey, my editor Laura Godwin, the illustrator Beatriz Gutierrez, and the entire publishing team.

Before attempting to write these poems, I read numerous history books, diaries, and other firsthand accounts. In addition, one of the most comprehensive resources was the PBS series called *Latino Americans* and a companion book, *Latino Americans: The 500-Year Legacy That Shaped a Nation*, by Ray Suarez (Penguin, 2013). I am also indebted to *Our America: A Hispanic History of the United States*, by Felipe Fernández-Armesto (Norton, 2014), and *An Indigenous People's History of the United States*, by Roxanne Dunbar-Ortíz (Beacon Press, 2015).